D1614219

ISBN 10: 1490320970

ISBN 13: 978-1490320977

Printed in the United States of America

# Bird
## that wants to Fly

written by Diane Kaufman

illustrated by Olya Kalatsei

The bird that wants to fly was limping
along by the winter carnival.
She passed the "please enter" sign of
the roller coaster attraction, tail feathers
neatly tucked between her legs.
"Oh my," she sighed.
"Life is so long and dreary."

hat I am

Looking down, she came across a puddle.
It must have rained, but she hadn't noticed,
so preoccupied she was with yesterday's
miscalculations. As she put one foot in, as
she couldn't change direction, she noticed a
reflection ~ a magical horse with blue mascara,
the words, "beautiful animal that I am."

Although it hurt her neck to do so, she looked up. The blue eyed horse with the pink mane, was only a few inches away. The bird made the tiniest chirp. And beautiful animal that I am heard her.

She said, "Little bird why are you walking not flying? Doesn't it take longer that way?"
The bird paused in her steps and grew thoughtful. She was so used to only her own company that all this came as a surprise. She cleared her throat with three chirps and replied, "I used to know how to fly."
"You did?" said beautiful animal. "What happened?"
"It's a long sad story. Can you stay awhile?"

"Oh yes!" said beautiful horse. "I'm not in a hurry. I can stay here as long as you like. Oh! And would you like to rest on my back? You might be more comfortable, if your story is as long as you say."
"Horse! What a lovely suggestion! Why, thank you!"
And with that bird that wants to fly pulled herself up on the stirrups, hoisted herself upon the saddle, and rested her head on the pink mane of beautiful horse.

She had worked so hard her heart was pounding!
"Better rest a while" said beautiful animal.
And so the bird did.

When she opened her eyes it was evening.
She thought, "I must have been so tired and didn't know it.
I'm sure it must have been morning when I started to walk."

Beautiful animal was awake and said, "Tell me your story. I am so eager to know you."
Once again bird chirped and plucked up her courage.
"It's a story that is so long, that I better shorten it lest I forget where I was going."
"Here's the whole thing in one sentence."

"I was born to fly and I did fly and I have beautiful wings, but I was caught in snow storms and rainstorms, not to mention blizzards and freezing rain

and children with rocks and men with shot guns and other birds bumping and crashing and it goes on and on so I decided to walk."

Beautiful animal thought it over and this is what she said, "Want to go on the roller coaster with me? I know the owner and we can have a ride just us two." The lights of the roller coaster were dazzling and the "please enter" sign so inviting.

"Only one request please." said beautiful animal. "I want to see your beautiful wings. Won't you fly to the coaster's seat? It's just over there, not so far away. It's a good way to begin."

Little bird who wants to fly took a deep breath, and with a loud and most beautiful chirp, spread her wings.

Our story ends with bird flying alone in the sky, but that is also just the beginning. What do you imagine happens next? Please feel free to draw and write your story on these pages. **Now go ahead and spread your wings!**